Britney Spears' Crossroads Diary

INTRODUCTION

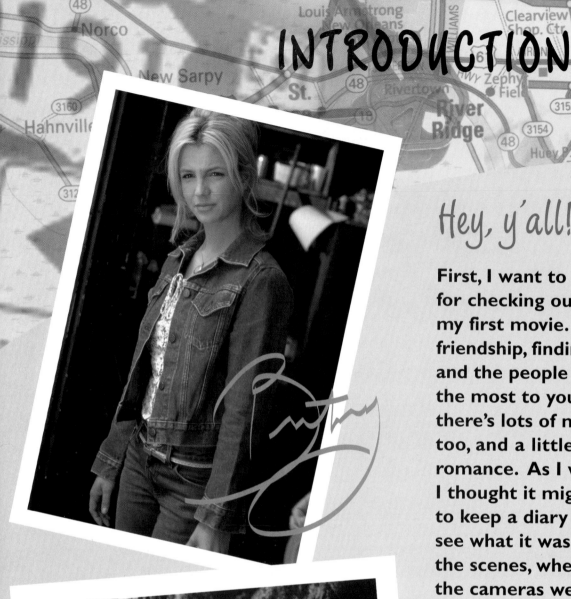

Hey, y'all!

First, I want to say thanks for checking out *Crossroads*, my first movie. It's all about friendship, finding yourself, and the people who mean the most to you. Of course, there's lots of music in it, too, and a little bit of romance. As I was filming, I thought it might be a kick to keep a diary so you could see what it was like behind the scenes, when the cameras weren't rolling. **Warning: It's a reality check!** You might find, like I did, that the glamour of being a movie star comes with . . . oh, crack-of-dawn wake-up calls, lots of dialogue to memorize, digging deep inside yourself to come up with emotions — and lots of mosquitoes.

Taryn, me, and Zoë having a time capsule moment

Yikes!

4

Britney Spears' Crossroads Diary

by Britney Spears and Felicia Culotta

SCHOLASTIC INC.

New York Toronto London Auckland Sydney

Mex   nos Aires

ISBN 0-439-39745-6

Designed by Robin Camera

12 11 10 9 8 7 6 5 4 3   2 3 4 5 6 7/0

Printed in the U.S.A.
First Scholastic printing, February 2002

MEET MY NEW FRIENDS — THE CAST

Before I start, I want to introduce the main characters and the actors who star in *Crossroads* along with me.

I play Lucy, an only child who lives with her dad, Pete, in a small town in Georgia. Lucy's parents got divorced when she was much younger, and her mom lives out in Arizona. They don't communicate.

Lucy is the kind of girl who doesn't make waves. She's spent her whole life following the path her dad has laid out for her. She's smart and gets good grades; she's planning to be a doctor. But she really loves to sing and to write. She's a poet and is kind of obsessive about her journal.

Zoë Saldana plays Kit. She's rich and popular, and when the movie starts, a really snobby type who's engaged to her high school sweetheart, Dylan. He goes to college in California.

Taryn Manning plays Mimi. The opposite of Kit, she's from the poor side of town and has had a really rough time of it. Everyone in school considers her an outsider.

Kit

Mimi

 Lucy

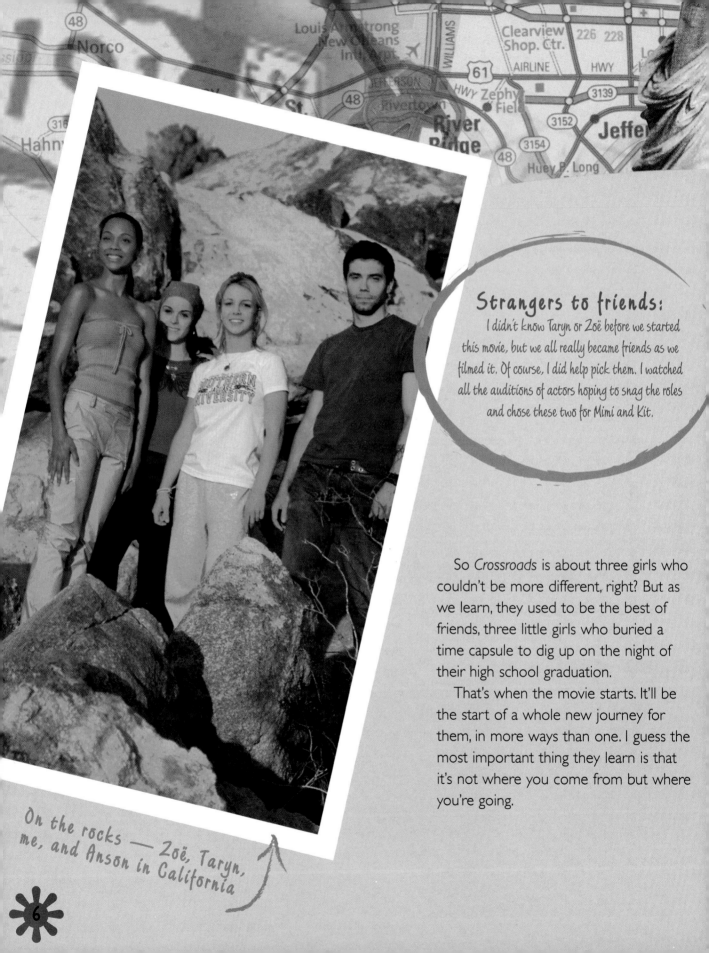

Strangers to friends:

I didn't know Taryn or Zoë before we started this movie, but we all really became friends as we filmed it. Of course, I did help pick them. I watched all the auditions of actors hoping to snag the roles and chose these two for Mimi and Kit.

So *Crossroads* is about three girls who couldn't be more different, right? But as we learn, they used to be the best of friends, three little girls who buried a time capsule to dig up on the night of their high school graduation.

That's when the movie starts. It'll be the start of a whole new journey for them, in more ways than one. I guess the most important thing they learn is that it's not where you come from but where you're going.

On the rocks — Zoë, Taryn, me, and Anson in California

And speaking of that, someone pretty special was with me the whole time we filmed *Crossroads*. Felicia Culotta — we call her Fe — has been close to me since I first started doing music. She's been my guardian, but now she's my assistant and close friend. Since I was so busy making the movie, I asked her to help me with the diary.

Secret! Don't tell:

Anson Mount is so perfect for the role of Ben. When Fe and I went to see him, he was in character for another movie he was doing at the time. That film was so unlike **Crossroads**, we just couldn't picture him in the role of Ben. But luckily, folks with more casting foresight than we had **could**, and he got the role. He's rugged looking, with a very endearing warmth underneath. I think y'all will agree, he did a beautiful job!

Anson

7

home
sweet
home!

Crossroads was born in the middle of a store. There's a place in Los Angeles called Fred Segal, where I love to shop. One day, me and Fe were hanging out there when I blurted something I'd been thinking about for a long time. Fe remembers me saying, "Oooh, I'd really love to do a movie!" But not just any movie. I wanted to do something different, something that felt real and important to me. I had been reading a whole bunch of scripts that other people had sent me. Nothing struck my fancy, nothing felt right.

I'm all about the friendship vibe. So I wanted that to be the main theme. And I've always loved the idea of a road trip. That was something I really wanted to be part of the movie.

I spoke to one of my managers, Larry, and he hooked me up with Ann, a movie producer, who introduced me to a screenwriter named Shonda. She wrote the HBO movie *Introducing Dorothy Dandridge*, which starred Halle Berry. Shonda and I actually spent our first afternoon back at Fred Segal, just talking. Not about the movie, really. It was more Shonda getting to know me. In fact, she did more observing and listening than actual talking.

An unusual way to write a movie, you might think, but it worked. She got the feel of where I was at, she picked up on exactly what my vision was. After that, she set about writing. We would talk every once in a while, but mainly, Shonda got it. She got me, and she wrote a script.

Best of all, we made sure some of the movie could be filmed in Louisiana, where I'm from and where my family lives. It's where I feel most comfortable *and* I could go home every night while we filmed there.

So hop in the car with us and strap on your seat belt. It's gonna be a fun but definitely bouncy trip!

Reality ✔:
Louisiana "stunt doubled" for most of the states our characters drive through in the movie!

THE FIRST DAY

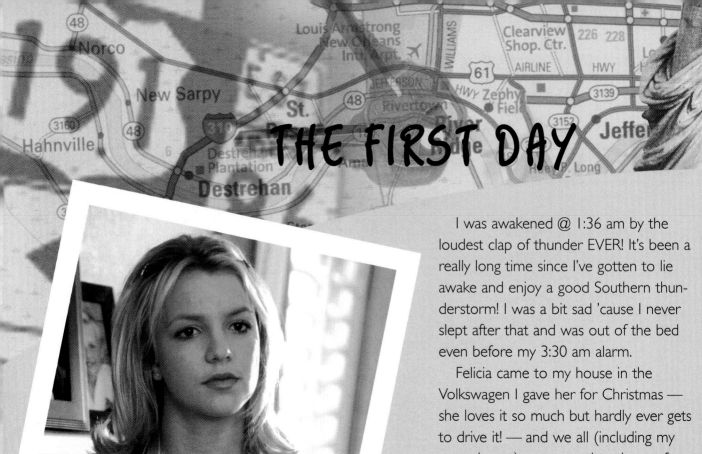

I was awakened @ 1:36 am by the loudest clap of thunder EVER! It's been a really long time since I've gotten to lie awake and enjoy a good Southern thunderstorm! I was a bit sad 'cause I never slept after that and was out of the bed even before my 3:30 am alarm.

Felicia came to my house in the Volkswagen I gave her for Christmas — she loves it so much but hardly ever gets to drive it! — and we all (including my mom, Lynne) caravanned to the set for our 1st shooting day. Got here a little after 5 am. We parked right across the railroad tracks in downtown Hammond, Louisiana.

I went straight into hair and makeup, then to the wardrobe trailer to put on my Lucy clothes. Fe calls them "casual frumpy" — jeans, sneakers, cotton button-down shirt under a sweatshirt. Accessorized with a yellow canvas pocketbook and a bucket cap. They're the opposite of what I usually wear.

The first scene we're shooting is the four of us — me, Taryn, Zoë, and Anson Mount, who plays Ben, in this cool old car! It's a 1974 yellow convertible Cutlass.

Film factoid:

Sides are a pullout of the lines we need to memorize for that day's shoot only, printed on a little half sheet of paper you can keep in your pocket.

I'm a bit quiet today — due to lack of sleep! But I'm glad it's not raining!

Finally got to take a much-needed nap — me and Mom both — and I know EXACTLY why they call them "power naps"! I feel *much* better.

In spite of some more thunderclaps, we were able to shoot all the rest of the day and into sunset. We went home *very* tired and *very* fulfilled. I learned so much! I learned to read *sides*.

Went to sleep @ 9:10 pm!
Good first day!

Second reality ✔:
We filmed the movie out of sequence. So the first scene we actually shot — this one — doesn't come until much later in Crossroads.

11

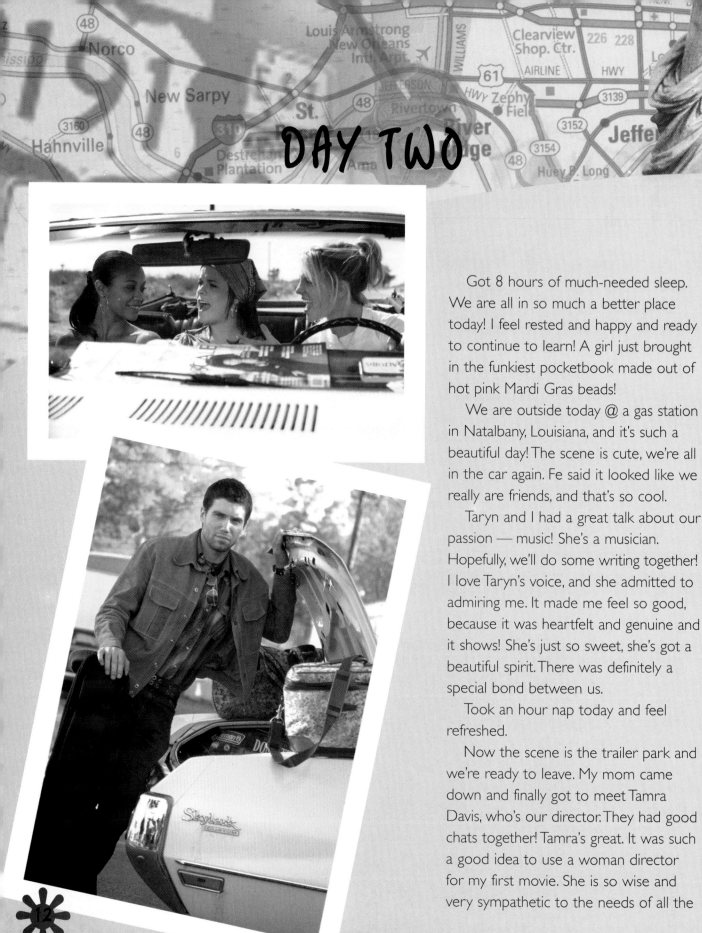

Got 8 hours of much-needed sleep. We are all in so much a better place today! I feel rested and happy and ready to continue to learn! A girl just brought in the funkiest pocketbook made out of hot pink Mardi Gras beads!

We are outside today @ a gas station in Natalbany, Louisiana, and it's such a beautiful day! The scene is cute, we're all in the car again. Fe said it looked like we really are friends, and that's so cool.

Taryn and I had a great talk about our passion — music! She's a musician. Hopefully, we'll do some writing together! I love Taryn's voice, and she admitted to admiring me. It made me feel so good, because it was heartfelt and genuine and it shows! She's just so sweet, she's got a beautiful spirit. There was definitely a special bond between us.

Took an hour nap today and feel refreshed.

Now the scene is the trailer park and we're ready to leave. My mom came down and finally got to meet Tamra Davis, who's our director. They had good chats together! Tamra's great. It was such a good idea to use a woman director for my first movie. She is so wise and very sympathetic to the needs of all the

Anson and me doing a scene together!

girls. She's directed lots of videos and movies, including *Billy Madison*.

I worked with my acting coach, Belita, for the rest of the day. She is fabulous. I requested that she stay on set with me the whole time, to help me. It was such a treat to have her. Even when I didn't need the help so much later on, it made me feel confident to know she was there.

What you didn't see on camera:

During filming, we made Anson stop the car and pick up 2 stray puppies! They were itty-bitty things on the side of the road. Anson didn't think it was cute at all! But three girls outnumbered him. Our crew found good homes for them.

13

DAY THREE

✳ Dan Aykroyd — he'll be playing Lucy's dad, Pete, in the movie

Had a little later call today and it felt so nice not leaving home in the dark! Fe met up with us in Kenwood, and we talked all the way to the set. Got to the set about the same time as all the mosquitoes! UGH! Big Rob — he's been my bodyguard for three years — and Phil, our videographer, got eaten up!

My spirits are good! All this "home" is so good for the soul! Fe gave Anson a Motorola pager since he was entranced with ours and we had some extras. We warned him how much he was going to love it!

We all loaded up in vans — me, Anson, Tamra, and lots of camera equipment rode together — to get the next shot for the movie, which is me and Anson (Lucy and Ben, of course) getting to know each other in the car.

The mosquitoes are AWFUL!! Good thing we travel with a medic — on tour, too — who's spraying us all down.

Larry just called and told my mom that he wants her here when I see the *dailies* (that's the film footage of what we do today or each day). He's scared I'll be my own worst critic, so he thought it would be better if my mom were there with me.

Seeing yourself acting on film is strange — but I came away feeling really good about the shoot so far today! Ate yummy tuna salad for lunch and then napped.

Fe reminded me that I needed to call Dan Aykroyd — he'll be playing Lucy's dad, Pete, in the movie — when I wake up! (I did and had a great chat!)

Film factoid:
Just learned that the **picture car**, the one that we are driving, is on top of the **process trailer**, which is pulled by the **insert truck**. Love to learn something new daily!

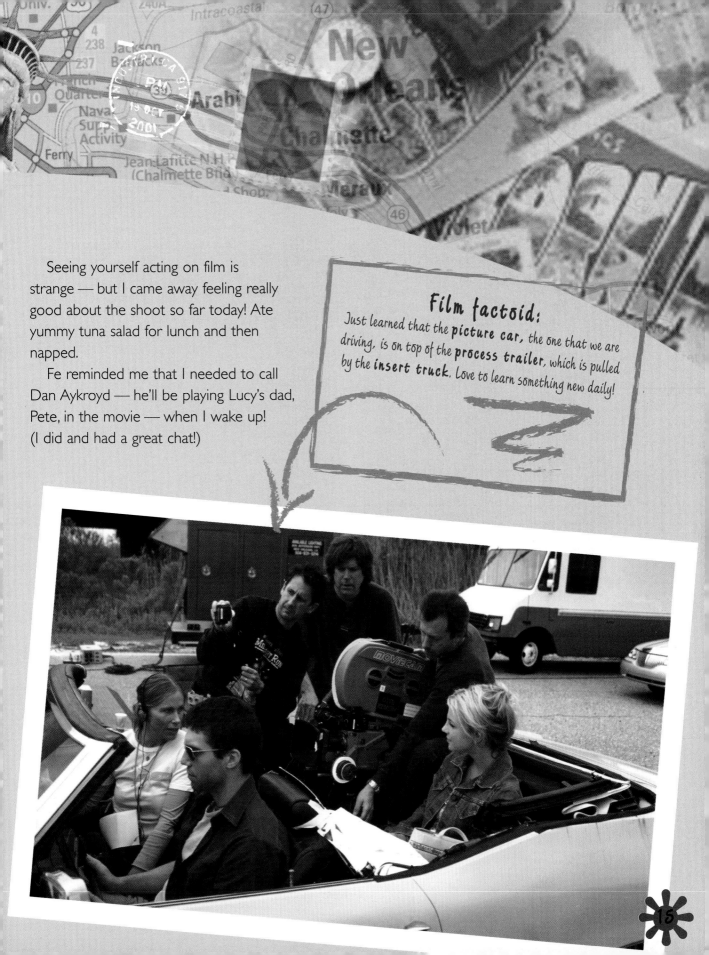

DAY FOUR

We zoomed home last night to beat the thunderstorms! Lots of lightning streaked the sky — it was sort of exciting to anticipate a storm. Laughed all the way to Kenwood, with Fe, Rob, Phil, and Mom. Got up early (4:45) and arrived early (6:35!!). All of us sort of quiet!! And a bit out of sorts.

Phil and Fe were kidding around all day. Phil was trying to get Fe to say the word "trashy," but she kept refusing. So he just kept asking and asking, and finally she socked him with just about the wimpiest punch ever. We were all cracking up.

Then there was me and Bryan, my older brother. I have a really nice friendship with him. He's always coming to me for advice about girls. Like, "Why does she act like that?" Usually, I take the girl's side! But today I had the guilts for telling him what I really felt, even though it was the truth!

Today is the scene where the girls fight!! Lots of dialogue and acting!! I rehearsed in the trailer first and then rehearsed again on set. Zoë ran from Taryn in the first fight scene. Taryn never backed down or got out of character! I jumped down from the car, threw my script down, and went right into the scene! Even better than the rehearsal — I was feeling it! Fe said we looked so natural!

We're on set — done with rehearsals and on to filming. The first take went GREAT! Tamra came over with constructive help — she told me not to lean on the car when I deliver Lucy's "mad" speech — she feels Lucy would actually be too mad to just lean as she was screaming. I totally appreciated and agreed with her advice!

Now on to touch up and next take! Just found out — our call for tomorrow (Fri) is @ 5:15 am in Baton Rouge! UGH — I'm tired just thinking about it.

After our shooting day, Mom, Fe, Phil, and I went out for a coffee. Then home to sleep!

ZZZZZZ...

17

Got up @ 3:30 am to meet Rob and Felicia for our 6:00 am call time in Baton Rouge! Made it here early and was so happy! Felt sick in my belly cause it's so early.

Phil and Felicia just ran to Wal-Mart for Belita's idea: Belita will read my lines for the next day into the tape recorder two or three different ways, like putting the accent on different words in the sentence. Then I can pick which one I feel best about. It helps me familiarize myself w/ all of them for the next day! Good Idea!

Phil is all excited because I decided I want him to do my *MTV Diary* show, a behind-the-scenes videography of making this movie.

All going well today! We're at a gas station, and the scene is where Taryn and I (Mimi and Lucy) are fighting about Lucy wanting to leave. We played a good ol' parking lot game of Wiffle ball after lunch! There were spectators to cheer us on! Felicia thought she was bad till Anson came! HA! No — Taryn was the best.

I got coffee from a cute camera assistant and decided that he needed to be Felicia's boyfriend! HA! Fe thinks he's so uninterested!?

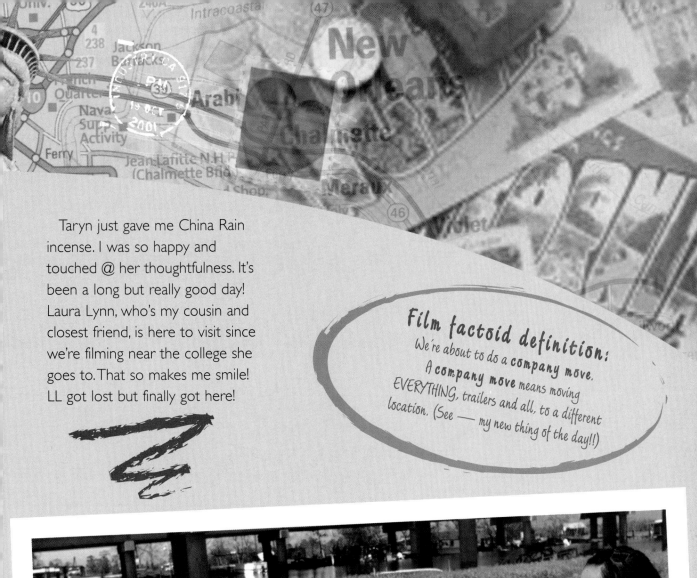

Taryn just gave me China Rain incense. I was so happy and touched @ her thoughtfulness. It's been a long but really good day! Laura Lynn, who's my cousin and closest friend, is here to visit since we're filming near the college she goes to. That so makes me smile! LL got lost but finally got here!

Film factoid definition:
We're about to do a **company move**. A **company move** means moving EVERYTHING, trailers and all, to a different location. (See — my new thing of the day!!)

DAY SIX

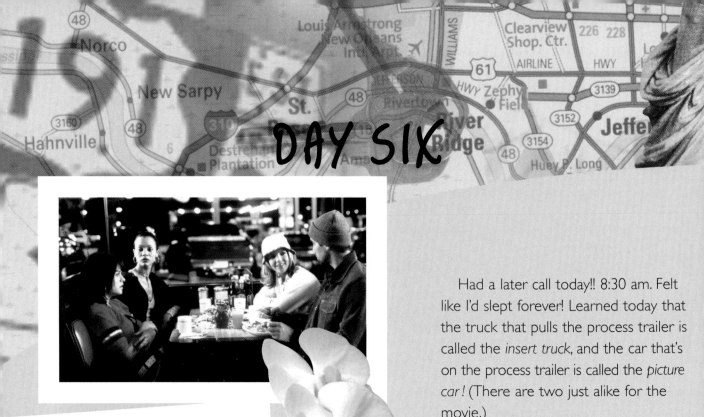

Orchids for
Michael Jackson

Had a later call today!! 8:30 am. Felt like I'd slept forever! Learned today that the truck that pulls the process trailer is called the *insert truck*, and the car that's on the process trailer is called the *picture car*! (There are two just alike for the movie.)

I ordered orchids for Michael Jackson. The card read "It would have been an honor to be there and be with you on a day when everyone was honoring you. Can't wait to see you. You'll be in my prayers! Love, Britney." I ordered them from Gary's store in NYC to be delivered to the room of MJ's assistant, Frank, today! I bet he calls! COOL!

Today is St. Patrick's Day and Anson wore his green boxers — just to be safe! This day's scene is where all 4 of us are in the car — just scenic stuff. Then we do a company move to the Waffle House for the scenes there. Lucy has lots of lines in that scene. Anson so far has eaten 3 plates of food. Fe says I seem quite comfortable with all this movie stuff — I think she's right. Jamie, my little sister, brought Big Rob an oyster po'boy, and we all took a bite! It was great!

Now the boys are outside playin' Wiffle ball and yelling and screaming.

Cool stuff I learned:

Camera Shots

Single — just one person

Close-up — CU

2-shot — 2 people in shot

Wide shot — (WS) (Master) — establishing shot
(example: camera across street shoots Waffle House to
show where they are)

Over the shoulder — see bit of hair and back of other
person

1st team — cast

2nd team — stand-ins

NEW ORLEANS!
(HALFWAY THROUGH!)

Today we had a call time of 9:30 am! It felt so good to have had a day off and then a later call time! I wrote a cute (Dido-sounding) song @ hair and makeup, and when I sang it to Felicia she made me record it on my Belita recorder for use @ another time! Rode down with the cast to the causeway in a 15-pas (15-passenger van).

Just got out of the car (*follow car*) — Felicia took a pic of me with a traffic cone on my head! Goofball!!

Just got to the French Quarter — a section of New Orleans. Our set is a beautiful courtyard. Me, Taryn, and Mimi are in pj's, chatting about our night out. Just did our first real take and all went well. The day is Great! After we wrapped, Fe and me went to a little café and relaxed w/ Zoë, Anson, Taryn, and Phil. Listened to old jukebox music, and Wendy (from wardrobe) came by and danced with Zoë. Fun night!

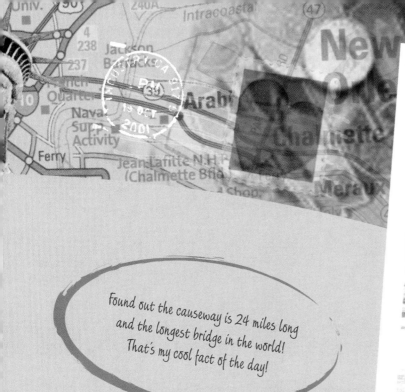

Found out the causeway is 24 miles long
and the longest bridge in the world!
That's my cool fact of the day!

LOS ANGELES!

Reality:

Just like Louisiana stunt doubled for all the states our characters drive through, Los Angeles, California, is where we shot all the interior scenes. In other words, every time you see us indoors — clubs, hotel rooms, Lucy's mom's house, onstage performing — that was all done in a Los Angeles studio. That's partly why **Crossroads** was filmed out of sequence. We did all the exterior or outdoor scenes first, then all the indoor scenes.

Flew back to L.A. yesterday! Good flight. Felicia asked the flight attendant to heat up her food — leftovers from her sister's home cooking. She just thought that it would be better than airline food! Rob and I laughed so hard! Lance Bass (*N Sync) just called from his movie set in Toronto to wish me good luck with *Crossroads*! So sweet!

Now I have to get dressed for my scene today. No lines, just the four of us getting ready for the talent show auditions! They've got me walking in the middle of a street. Rob, my bodyguard, is going nuts! (Guess he's worried I'll be recognized.)

We were each given our director's chair today — you know, those canvas chairs with your name stitched on the back — and they're so cute! We are all so proud! (My first director's chair!)

The extras for this scene are so great. Jesse Camp, former MTV/VJ, is making a cameo and is so excited.

DAY TWO IN LOS ANGELES

UGH! Another early morning —
5:15 am pickup. Slept most of the way
here. We're on location in Lancaster,
CA, about 1 1/2 hours from Los Angeles.
All of us are a bit unmotivated
today. Guess it's the early call. Right
now, we're @ a gas station, and the
scene is when we girls "steal" Ben's car ♥

Today, Kim Cattrall (*Sex and the City*) did her scene. She plays my mom. She was just as I'd expected — so sweet, pretty, professional, and FOCUSED! I was blown away! It was like we clicked immediately! Kim worked so hard and asked Belita lots of questions. She made me feel really good that she cared so much! Fe took pictures of me and Kim and promised to send them to her. She so looked like she could be related to me.

Next Day. Got up early again and still managed to be 30 minutes late! We're way out here in the desert for sure.

I am in a super mood. My mom and my little sister, Jamie Lynn, and her friend Krystal are visiting today, and we all played hide-and-seek. Those girls amazed me with their hiding abilities! They hid at the top of the closet in my trailer, hanging from the bar like a couple of monkeys. I couldn't see them at all. They really cracked me up.

GUEST STAR 2:
DAN AYKROYD

What a slacker I am! It's been DAYS since I've written. Today is Phil's 19th birthday. We plan to treat him really special.

I'm working with Dan Aykroyd today. He is so into his part, too. He's got a buzz cut and a fake tattoo of a submarine.

Tamra just showed me a video of actress-singer Ann-Margret in the old movie *Bye Bye Birdie* — she was dressing and changing clothes while singing. That helped in the scene where Lucy had to do the same thing — Fe says I totally ACED that scene! It was cute. I sang and danced and plopped on the bed with my butt!

Phil just got Dodgers baseball opening-day tickets from Jive (our record label) and is so happy! Hopefully, he can hook up with Anson and go enjoy the game.

Dan Aykroyd seems to be enjoying himself and is so into the scene and his character.

Cool stuff I learned today:

A **soft flag** (attached to a tall stand) softens the light

A **hard flag** cuts off to direct the lights

Barn doors are flaps attached to either side of the light to direct the
light. This is what hit me on the head at the "...Oops I Did It Again" shoot!

Motion picture is a picture that moves!

THE BEGINNING OF THE END

Early call! On set @ 5 am for hair and makeup. Worse than usual since we stayed out a bit late last night to celebrate Fe's birthday. A whole bunch of us went, including Zoë, Anson, and Taryn — we ate out and went dancing. Fun!

Only now it's really cold on the set! And we're all tired.

We filmed the ending part today and it seemed melancholy. It's the part where Lucy gets out of the car and decides to stay in California with Ben. We're filming right across the street from Mann's Chinese Theater — it's a cool sight!

Oops alert:
Here's something you'll never see on camera: The crew was setting up the lights in the hotel — they got too hot and the smoke alarms went off, and the sprinkler system came on and flooded the place!
UGH!

Filming with Anson in Los Angeles

FRIDAY IN L.A.

Later call today — 7:30 am. All's well. Today's shooting is just me and Dan. First @ the repair shop — this is one of the first scenes in the movie — and then @ the hospital, one of the last scenes in the movie. (See what I mean by shooting this film out of sequence?)

You'd think this would be confusing for the actors, but not so much. I'm happy and rested and so enjoying working with Dan. He seems pretty pumped to be working on this movie as well.

Had more company today, friends from home.

MONDAY

Early call today — 5:30 am! — but after a good weekend, all feels good about being back on the set. And I'm in a great mood after a fun/relaxing Justin weekend.

We're shooting in a school hallway — oh, the ... *Baby, One More Time* FLASH-BACKS!

The guy playing Henry is so perfect for this part. His real name is Justin, and he's on the TV show *Ed.* I enjoyed getting to know him for the short time we worked together. We're @ school right before the graduation ceremony starts.

Kit (Zoë) runs into me (Lucy) in the hall and knocks my books out of my hands and then taunts me for being such a "good" girl.

Had yummy meals from *craft services.*

Film factoid:
Craft services means the catering company — they provide all the food on movie sets.

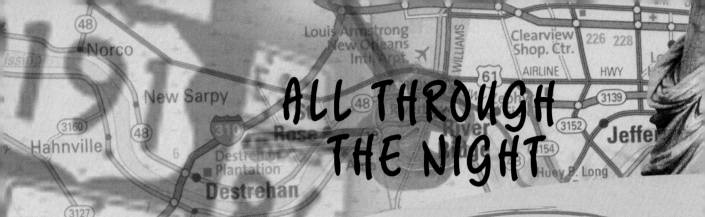

Reality ✔:

I found out one reason it takes so long to make a movie. They shoot the same scene over and over again from different camera angles — at least three or four takes per scene!

5:30 pm call, which only means an ALL-NIGHT shoot! We all are over this day already! We were over an hour late. UGH! Fe and I had good van chats as we followed the process trailer. Now we're on to the next setup, after a company move to a supermarket setting.

I'm excited about leaving the set and heading straight for the airport and on to Justin's for Easter. We were supposed to leave the set around 4 am but didn't until 5 am. **Ugh!**

AN OLD HOTEL

WOW! It's been so long since I've written —
everything's been crazy-busy with all those night
shots. Body so out of sync. But we're working @
the coolest old Hollywood hotel. It's called the
Ambassador. It's the hotel where the old-time movie
stars like Frank Sinatra hung out in a club called the
Coconut Grove. It got really spooky @ night. It has
800 EMPTY rooms! The groundskeeper said there's
at least a movie a week filmed here. The reason it
closed down was there were no sprinklers and
there was asbestos, so to refurbish it would have
cost way too much.

THE HARDEST SCENES

I'm sitting by myself, trying to get sad. It's the scene where Lucy comes back to the hotel in the pouring rain after her mom treats her so poorly. She cries. I'll admit these were the hardest scenes for me. How did I do it? I remembered things that made me sad, but mostly I just put myself in Lucy's place. I thought about how I'd feel if my mom didn't love me, and I just hurt for her. Feeling the way Lucy would feel brought on the tears.

Felicia feels so bad for me. I can tell that it breaks her heart to watch me getting so upset. She's a real friend, that's for sure.

She's right about something else, too. She told me that she can see me getting more confident about acting. It's true. I'm less worried about all this movie stuff — sometimes I even feel like an old pro! I'm relaxed and secure.

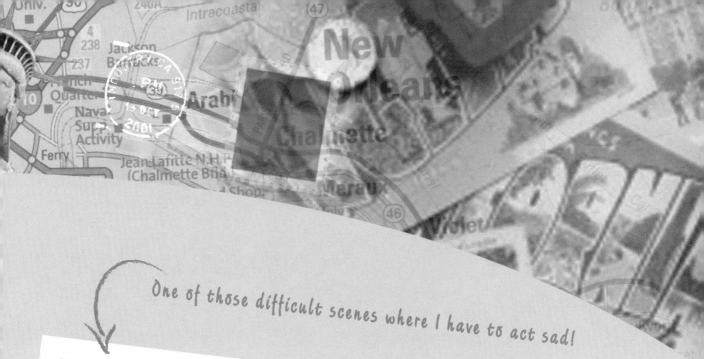

One of those difficult scenes where I have to act sad!

Back at the Ambassador Hotel. We didn't start on time, 'cause I had to talk to Clive, the Chairman/CEO of Jive, my record company. I felt strongly about this song, "Bombastic Love," *not* being used in the screen version, only on the DVD version. It took me a long time to talk him out of it. But I walked away satisfied that we're not gonna use it as a single release from my new album.

The scene we're shooting right now is when we walk into a hotel room and Zoë — I mean Kit! — is so snobby and refuses to stay. She says it looks kinky. Then she sits on the bed and it collapses!

I broke out into fits of REAL laughter!

Film factoid:
Wild track means
off-camera audio.

PRETENDING

Got a full 8 hours of sleep last night! Felt good coming to work. Of course everyone noticed I was all smiles and glowing — just from my phone chat with Justin!

We're back on the set and the scene we're doing is when Lucy's showering and the girls keep bothering her. During our breaks, Zoë and I are having some real good chats.

I'm now doing another one of those really hard scenes. I'm crying and talking to Anson (Ben). It's very emotional. I couldn't pick my spirits up afterward. I know Felicia wanted to help me smile, but she couldn't. I did so well with my crying that Fe couldn't even watch! She thought it would make her way too sad. But I feel good about my performance — just really drained.

Reality ✔:

The most uncomfortable part of acting in **Crossroads**? It's pretending to be in love with someone when you're really in love with someone else! Felicia actually remembers me coming into the trailer after a romance scene and going, "Ooh! I can't believe I just did that!" Don't get me wrong. Anson is a great person, and we have a good friendship, but there's no real attraction. Hopefully, we're good enough actors that the audience will never know that.

KARAOKE TIME

We're at this cool place called Fais Do Do. It's soooo New Orleans even though of course we're in Los Angeles. We're filming the part where we enter a karaoke contest to win $ to fix the car. See? I told you *Crossroads* was totally filmed out of sequence!

This was a scene where all my friends — Fe included — got to be in the "audience" and have a great time. They did the bump to the song "I Love Rock 'n' Roll" by Joan Jett. Everyone left smiling and in great spirits!

Off camera, I have been working on music — some new stuff with Josh and Bryan, the songwriters and producers on my new album. Clive and Barry, the president of my record company, came to watch the movie being shot and then stayed over the weekend to listen to our new music. We had some long chats!

MONDAY

Back to this early am stuff. UGH! We got a call from our publicity person at Jive, Sonia, who said she'd saved this photo session I did for *Vogue* magazine. Yeah!! Now that everyone's camera-ready, onto the set we go!

We're at another place, called Club Bayou, and they're reshooting the karaoke scene, this time from Lucy, Kit, and Mimi's angle. It's sounding great, and all of us are REALLY into it!

Reality ✔:
Lucy's the daughter of an auto mechanic and knows all about car repair. Me? Let's just say that on a recent road escapade with Felicia, it took the two of us 20 minutes to figure out how to put gas in the car!

A FRIEND IN THE AUDIENCE

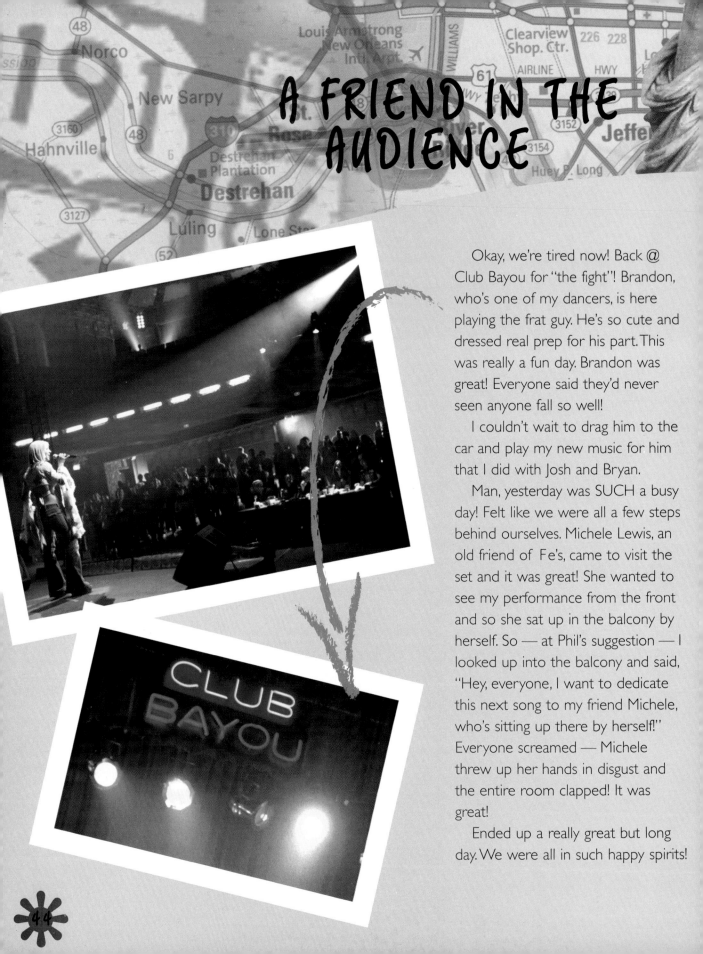

Okay, we're tired now! Back @ Club Bayou for "the fight"! Brandon, who's one of my dancers, is here playing the frat guy. He's so cute and dressed real prep for his part. This was really a fun day. Brandon was great! Everyone said they'd never seen anyone fall so well!

I couldn't wait to drag him to the car and play my new music for him that I did with Josh and Bryan.

Man, yesterday was SUCH a busy day! Felt like we were all a few steps behind ourselves. Michele Lewis, an old friend of Fe's, came to visit the set and it was great! She wanted to see my performance from the front and so she sat up in the balcony by herself. So — at Phil's suggestion — I looked up into the balcony and said, "Hey, everyone, I want to dedicate this next song to my friend Michele, who's sitting up there by herself!" Everyone screamed — Michele threw up her hands in disgust and the entire room clapped! It was great!

Ended up a really great but long day. We were all in such happy spirits!

Right before I embarrass Michele! — It was GREAT !

IT'S ALMOST OVER

Today is another good day. The whole scene is riding on my performance. We all love the outfits, and I'm singing "Overprotected." Anson is on the keyboards and there's an actual band called the Unknowns playing with him. It's real cool. I can totally see this in show form now.

It's $5 Friday. That's where you write your name on a $5 bill and they draw @ the end of the day and whoever is picked gets it all.

It's so weird that this is almost the last day of shooting. It's DONE on Monday.

OUR LAST DAY!

Felicia tried to avoid everyone. She just hates to say bye. I was very quiet and melancholy.

We'd decided to give everyone little good-bye gifts. I gave all the girls Lottie Dottie tote bags since they admired Felicia's. I also gave some people scented candles. Felicia surprised me with a book of pictures she took all during the filming. I loved it!

The wardrobe girls are selling all the extra stuff dirt cheap. I guess it's easier than packing it all up.

Me and Taryn and Zoë sang "I'm Not a Girl, Not Yet a Woman," and then took a cool group photo. And then . . . I broke down and cried. For real.

We all just needed to go quickly! So . . . **NO LONG GOOD-BYES!**

Wrap party at
House of Blues
tonight, given
by Dan Aykroyd!
See ya there!